HELLO READING books are a perfect introduction to reading. Brief sentences full of word repetition and full-color pictures stress visual clues to help a child take the first important steps toward reading. Mastering these story books will build children's reading confidence and give them the enthusiasm to stand on their own in the world of words."
—Bee Cullinan
Past President of the International Reading
Association, Professor in New York University's
Early Childhood and Elementary Education Program

Readers aren't born, they're made. Desire is planted—planted by parents who work at it."
—Jim Trelease
author of *The Read Aloud Handbook*

When I was a classroom reading teacher, I recognized the importance of good stories in making children understand that reading is more than just recognizing words. I saw that children who have ready access to story books get excited about reading. They also make noticeably greater gains in reading comprehension. The development of the HELLO READING stories grows out of this experience."
—Harriet Ziefert
M.A.T., New York University School of Education
Author, Language Arts Module,
Scholastic Early Childhood Program

For A.M.B., again and again

PUFFIN BOOKS
Published by the Penguin Group
Viking Penguin Inc., 40 West 23rd Street, New York, New York 10010, U.S.A.
Penguin Books Ltd, 27 Wrights Lane, London W8 5TZ, England
Penguin Books Australia Ltd, Ringwood, Victoria, Australia
Penguin Books Canada Ltd, 2801 John Street, Markham, Ontario, Canada L3R 1B4
Penguin Books (N.Z.) Ltd, 182-190 Wairau Road, Auckland 10, New Zealand

Penguin Books Ltd, Registered Offices: Harmondsworth, Middlesex, England

First published in Puffin Books, 1989 • Published simultaneously in Canada

1 3 5 7 9 10 8 6 4 2

Text copyright © Harriet Ziefert, 1989
Illustrations copyright © Mavis Smith, 1989
All rights reserved
Library of Congress catalog card number: 88-62146
ISBN 0-14-050980-1

Printed in Singapore for Harriet Ziefert, Inc.

Harry Goes
To Fun Land

Harriet Ziefert
Pictures by Mavis Smith

PUFFIN BOOKS

Harry went to Fun Land
with his grandpa.

Harry rode
the ferris wheel.
"I'm not scared,"
he said.

Harry rode
the bumper cars.

BUMP!

Harry even rode
the roller coaster.

"I'm not scared," he yelled.

Harry went
into the fun house.
It was dark—very dark.

n not scared," said Harry.

Harry looked into
funny mirrors.

Oh, my!
Oh, gosh!
Oh, no!

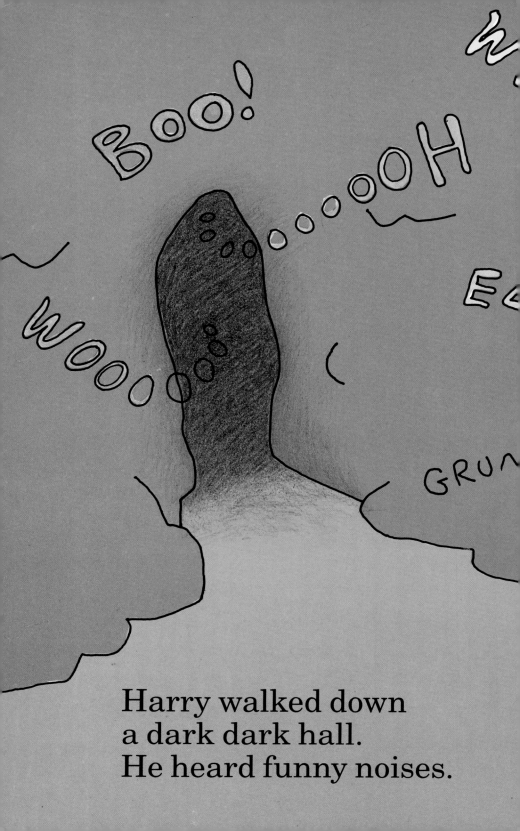

Harry walked down
a dark dark hall.
He heard funny noises.

Harry rode on
a magic carpet.

Soon he was
out of the dark and...

outside the fun house.

"I'm not scared," said Harry.
"I'm hungry!"

Harry ate popcorn...

and peanuts...

and cotton candy.

"Now I'm thirsty," said Harry.

"Wait here," said Grandpa.
"I'll get you a drink."

Harry sat and waited.

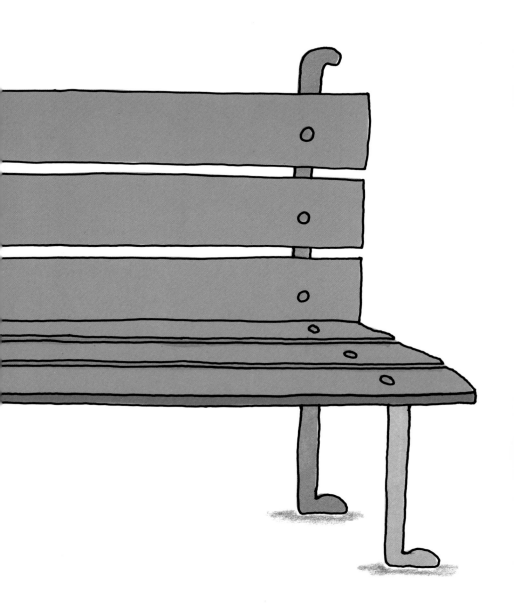

He waited and waited
and waited.

"I'm not scared,"
said Harry.
"Grandpa will be back soon."

"I'm back!" said Grandpa.
"You weren't scared, were you?"

"Who me? Scared?"
said Harry.
"Not anymore!"